# Where Does the Teacher Live?

by Paula Kurzband Feder
pictures by Lillian Hoban

PUFFIN BOOKS

PUFFIN BOOKS
Published by the Penguin Group
Penguin Books USA Inc., 375 Hudson Street, New York, New York 10014, U.S.A.
Penguin Books Ltd, 27 Wrights Lane, London W8 5TZ, England
Penguin Books Australia Ltd, Ringwood, Victoria, Australia
Penguin Books Canada Ltd, 10 Alcorn Avenue, Toronto, Ontario, Canada M4V 3B
Penguin Books (N.Z.) Ltd, 182-190 Wairau Road, Auckland 10, New Zealand
Penguin Books Ltd, Registered Offices: Harmondsworth, Middlesex, England

First published in the United States of America by E. P. Dutton, 1979
Published in Puffin Books, 1992
Published in a Puffin Easy-to-Read edition, 1996

1 3 5 7 9 10 8 6 4 2

Text copyright © Paula Kurzband Feder, 1979
Illustrations copyright © Lillian Hoban, 1979
All rights reserved
Puffin® and Easy-to-Read® are registered trademarks of Penguin Books USA Inc.

THE LIBRARY OF CONGRESS HAS CATALOGED THE DUTTON EDITION AS FOLLOWS:
Feder, Paula Kurzband. Where does the teacher live?
(A Fat cat book)
Summary: Three children try to discover where their teacher lives.
[1. Teachers—Fiction. 2. School stories.]
I. Hoban, Lillian. II. Title. III. Series.
PZ7.F3113Wh [E] 78-13157 ISBN 0-525-42586-1

Puffin Easy-to-Read ISBN 0-14-038119-8
Printed in the United States of America

Reading Level 1.7

Crewe Primary Library

to my daughter, Sarah Eleanore

It was Monday morning.

The children in Class 2–3

were having their milk.

Alba was sitting next to

her best friend, Nancy.

"Nancy," said Alba,

"do you know where

Mrs. Greengrass lives?"

Mrs. Greengrass was

the teacher of Class 2–3.

"She lives in school," said Nancy.

"All the teachers live in school."

Willie was sitting behind them

"Oh no no no," said Willie.

"She lives in a house

just like we do."

Willie was the smartest boy

in the class.

"Maybe Willie is right," said Alba.

"Let's find out," said Willie.

"We can wait after school

and see where she goes."

"Oh, she won't ever come out,"

said Nancy.

At three o'clock,

Alba, Willie, and Nancy

waited in front of the school.

Mrs. Greengrass came out.

She did not see the children.

10

They were hiding

behind a big boxwood bush.

"See?" said Alba to Nancy.

"Willie was right.

Mrs. Greengrass does not

live in school."

They followed Mrs. Greengrass

down the street, across the avenue,

and along the park.

Then she crossed another street.

"My mother will not let me

cross any more streets," said Nancy.

"All right," said Alba.

"We can just watch."

A bus stopped.

Mrs. Greengrass got on.

The bus went up the street
and turned at the corner.

"She must live far away," said Alba.

"Maybe she lives in the country,"
said Nancy.

"Oh no," said Willie.

"That was a city bus.

She must live in the city."

"Maybe Willie is right," said Alba.

"This is fun," said Willie.

"Let's do it again tomorrow."

At three o'clock on Tuesday,
Alba, Willie, and Nancy
hid behind the boxwood bush
to wait for Mrs. Greengrass.

"Look," said Willie.

"She is walking the same way.

She is going to take the bus again."

17

They followed Mrs. Greengrass

down the street, across the avenue,

and along the park.

They watched her cross the street.

A bus went in front of her.

"I told you," said Willie.

Then the bus moved away.

Surprise!

Mrs. Greengrass was still there.

She was still walking.

"Willie," said Alba,

"you were wrong."

"Maybe she is not going home

today," said Willie.

"Maybe she can walk
to her house," said Alba.
"Maybe she can walk
ten miles," said Nancy.
"No one can walk ten miles,"
said Willie.
"Maybe she can," said Alba.
"You were wrong today.
She did not take the bus."
Mrs. Greengrass kept on walking.
She went around the corner.
They could not see her anymore.

The next day was Wednesday.

It was raining hard.

"Here comes Mrs. Greengrass,"
said Alba.

"She cannot walk home today,"
said Willie. "It is too wet."

Mrs. Greengrass came
down the steps.
She looked
to the left.
She looked
to the right.

Suddenly she put her hand up
in the air.

"Look," said Willie.

"A taxi is stopping for her."

Mrs. Greengrass got in the taxi.

Alba, Willie, and Nancy waited

to see which way the taxi went.

It went the same way as the bus.

"Mrs. Greengrass has many ways

of going home," said Willie.

"I know something," said Alba.

"Mrs. Greengrass lives

on the west side of the city.

This is the east side,

and she always goes the other way."

"I am getting all wet," said Nancy,

"and I am getting tired of this.

Tomorrow let us ask

Mrs. Greengrass where she lives."

"Oh no! Wait one more day," said Alba.

"This is a big mystery."

"And we are good detectives,"

said Willie.

"Okay, one more day," said Nancy.

So on Thursday,

Alba, Willie, and Nancy

waited for Mrs. Greengrass.

She came out of the school.

She just stood there.

She did not walk.

She did not get on a bus.

She did not take a taxi.

A blue car came up the street.

A woman was driving the car.

She said hello to Mrs. Greengrass.

"Mrs. Greengrass is getting
into the car," said Nancy.
The blue car drove away.
"It is not going the same way
as the bus and taxi," said Alba.

"It is not going the same way
that Mrs. Greengrass walked,"
said Willie.

"I am all mixed up," said Alba.

"Tomorrow we will ask
Mrs. Greengrass where she lives."

On Friday, Alba, Willie, and Nancy

were eating lunch.

Mrs. Greengrass came

into the lunchroom.

"Mrs. Greengrass!" they shouted.

The teacher came over to them.

"Mrs. Greengrass,

where do you live?" asked Alba.

"Do you live in school?" asked Nancy.

"Do you live in the city?"
asked Willie.

"So many questions,"
said Mrs. Greengrass.

"Why do you want to know?"

33

"We just wondered," said Alba.

"We followed you," said Willie.

"On Monday we saw you
take a bus."

"On Tuesday we saw you walk,"

said Nancy. "You walked

the same way as the bus."

"On Wednesday we saw you

take a taxi," said Willie.

"It went the same way as the bus."

"I live on the west side,"
said Mrs. Greengrass.
"See? I told you
she lived on the west side,"
said Alba to Willie.

36

"But yesterday you got a ride

in a car," said Nancy.

"The car went a different way,"

said Willie.

"You are good detectives,"

said Mrs. Greengrass.

"Yesterday my friend

drove me to her house for dinner."

She smiled.

"Today I am going home

another way.

Wait for me after school."

At three o'clock,

Alba, Willie, and Nancy

stood in front of the school.

"Maybe she will fly home

in a helicopter," said Nancy.

Mrs. Greengrass

came out of the school.

"Hello, children," she said.

A small truck stopped

in front of the school.

A man was driving the truck.

Mrs. Greengrass said,

"Children, this is my uncle,

Frank Greengrass.

He sells ice cream to the stores."

Frank Greengrass

climbed out of the truck.

He gave something

to Mrs. Greengrass.

Mrs. Greengrass

walked over to the children.

"Here are three
chocolate marshmallow
ice-cream pops," she said.
"You are all such good detectives."

And Alba, Nancy, Willie,

and Mrs. Greengrass went home

in the ice-cream truck.